Ebb & Flo

and the
Baby Seal

Jane Simmons

Margaret K. McElderry Books
New York London Toronto Sydney Singapore

For Cordy, Miggy,
and Max

Margaret K. McElderry Books
An imprint of Simon & Schuster Children's Publishing Division
1230 Avenue of the Americas
New York, New York 10020

First published in Great Britain in 2000 by Orchard Books
First U.S. edition, 2002
2 4 6 8 10 9 7 5 3
Printed in Singapore

Library of Congress Control Number: 00-109519
ISBN: 0-689-84368-2

Ebb sat and listened to the rain and the wind.
Pitter, patter, pitter, patter, pitter, patter, whoosh!

Ebb had eaten all her biscuits
and chewed her toy into little bits.
She wanted someone to play with.
Woof! said Ebb, but Flo was busy
painting.

Woof! said Ebb, but Bird was busy chatting
with the ducks.
Woof! said Ebb, but Mom was busy too.

So Ebb sat and listened to
the wind and the rain.

*Pitter, patter, pitter, patter,
pitter, patter, whoosh!*

Then she heard a cry from
the beach. *Wah! Wah!*

It was a baby seal! At last Ebb
had someone to play with.
They played on the sand.

They played in the waves.

They played in
the rock pools.

Ebb and the baby seal played all day long.

As it got later, Ebb began to feel hungry.
But when she set off for home, the baby
seal tried to follow.

Wah! Wah! the baby seal cried.

Ebb stopped. *Woof!* she barked.
Why wouldn't the baby seal go home?
Ebb went to fetch help.

Woof! barked Ebb.
Beep! said Bird.
"Shush!" said Mom. "We're busy!"
Woof! WOOF! barked Ebb again, even louder.

"What's the matter, Ebb?"
asked Flo.
WOOF! WOOF! WOOF!
barked Ebb until Flo and
Mom followed her . . .

. . . all the way down to the beach.
  "It's a baby seal," said Flo.
"Maybe she's hungry."
  "Maybe she's lost," said Mom.

Wah! Wah! cried the baby seal.
"She needs her mom!" said Flo.
"And I know where to find her,"
said Mom. "Follow me!"

Flo followed Mom, Ebb followed Flo,
and the baby seal followed Ebb.
Wah! went the baby seal.

Flo heaved on the oars as Mom pushed off.
Woof! said Ebb to the baby seal.
Wah! the baby seal cried back.

They rowed all the way out to Seal Island.
Woof! Woof! barked Ebb.
Wah! went the baby seal.

There were seals everywhere.
"Oh, no!" said Flo. "We'll
never find her mom!"
Ebb looked out to sea.

Suddenly Ebb saw a head
bobbing all alone.
Woof! Woof! WOOF!
Ebb barked as loud as she could.
Then they heard a loud *HOO!*
Wah! answered the baby seal.
"Ebb, you've found her mom!"
said Flo.

The baby seal and her mother
played together.
"Well done, Ebb," said Flo.
Woof! said Ebb.
Wah! Hoo! said the seals.
"Let's go home," said Mom.

That night, Ebb dreamed of the sea
and boats and seals.

*Pitter patter, pitter, patter, pitter, patter,
whoosh!*

And far away there came a *Wah! Hoo!* . . .
but Ebb was fast asleep.